Brimhall
Turns
Detective

Brimhall
Turns
Detective

JUDY DELTON

illustrations by

CHERIE R. WYMAN

Carolrhoda Books, Inc./Minneapolis

This edition first published 1991 by Carolrhoda Books, Inc.
Text copyright © 1983 by Judy Delton.
Illustrations copyright © 1983 by Carolrhoda Books, Inc.

Manufactured in the United States of America

LIBRARY OF CONGRESS CATALOGING IN PUBLICATION DATA

Delton, Judy.
  Brimhall turns detective.

  (Carolrhoda on my own books)
  Summary: Huge footprints in the snow cause
Brimhall the bear to try to identify and trap
the "monster."
  [1. Bears—Fiction. 2. Snow—Fiction.
3. Monsters—Fiction] I. Wyman, Cherie R., ill.
II. Title. III. Series.
PZ7.D388Bt 1983   [E]   82-9582
ISBN 0-87614-203-X

1 2 3 4 5 6 7 8 9 10 00 99 98 97 96 95 94 93 92 91

Contents

Chapter One

The snow was gently falling in the woods. Bear and his cousin Brimhall were playing chess in their living room.

"Do you hear someone at the door, Bear?" said Brimhall.

Bear was thinking about his next move. "Aha!" he said. "I think I am going to win!"

"I thought I heard a noise," said Brimhall. He got up to look. He pulled open the door. A gust of wind blew the snow into the living room. Brimhall looked to the left. He looked to the right. All he saw were the trees blowing in the wind. Then he looked down at the ground.

"Bear!" he yelled. "I think you had better come here!"

Bear came to the door and looked out. "I think I just beat you, Brimhall," he said.

"Forget about chess, Bear," said Brimhall. "Look at those tracks in the snow!"

Bear looked at the ground. The tracks were very large.

"They come right to the door," said Brimhall. "Right up to *our* door."

The two cousins stood in the doorway. They looked at the tracks for a long time.

Bear rubbed his chin. "I don't know an animal that large," he said.

"It's no one we know," said Brimhall. "I think there is a monster in the forest."

"Don't be silly, Brimhall," said Bear. "Maybe we have a new neighbor who came to call on us. We might not have heard him. The doorbell is broken, you know."

Brimhall set his foot in one of the tracks. "Why, this animal has feet three times the size of mine!" he said. "Bear, that means he is three times larger than we are!"

The cousins went inside. Brimhall
shut the door tightly and locked it.
Then he put the safety chain on it.

"We have to catch that animal, Bear.
He could be dangerous, you know.
Neither of us is safe!"

17

"Catch him, Brimhall?" said Bear. "How could we catch him?"

Brimhall was pacing the floor. "I'm thinking," he said.

Bear yawned. "I'm tired," he said. "Just keep the door locked, Brimhall. I'm going to bed. Good night."

"Good night, Bear," said Brimhall. "I'm going to stay up awhile."

Brimhall sat down in his favorite chair. The snow swirled around corners of the house. The wind whistled in the pines. Soon Brimhall dozed off. He dreamed of giant animals outside the door and of monsters looking in the windows. When he woke up, he went to the door and opened it a crack. He looked out at the footprints. They were slowly filling up with snow.

"Dear me," he said, rubbing his chin. "I don't believe the lock on this door is enough." Suddenly he snapped his claws. "I have it!" he said. "I will build an alarm!"

Brimhall went to the basement and got his tools. He worked long into the night.

Chapter Two

The next morning a loud crash awoke Brimhall. He leaped out of bed.

"Bear!" he shouted. "I have caught the giant animal! I caught the monster!"

Brimhall put on his bathrobe and slippers. He ran to the kitchen. Pots and pans were everywhere—on the floor and in the sink and on the counter. Bear was limping in the door.

"Where is he, Bear? Where is he?"

"Brimhall," said Bear. "Do you know anything about this?"

"It is my foolproof trap, Bear. I tied a string from the door to the cupboard. If someone opens the door, the string opens the cupboard, and the pots and pans fall out. To warn us, Bear. And someone did open the door. I heard it. My alarm worked!"

"*I* opened the door, Brimhall, to get the paper."

"Dear me," said Brimhall. He looked disappointed. "I was sure that we would see the monster."

Brimhall went to the door and untied the string. He opened the door and looked out.

"Look, Bear!" he said. "The animal has been here again! He was here and we missed him."

"The noise probably scared him away," said Bear.

"You shouldn't have opened the door," said Brimhall. Bear just glared at him.

While Brimhall studied the fresh tracks in the snow, Bear picked up the pots and pans. "Well, I am going to bake today," he said. He got out his flour and honey. He began to sing.

Brimhall frowned. "Bear, this is serious. We have to find out what kind of an animal is nearby. We may be dealing with a very dangerous beast, you know."

Bear didn't seem to hear. He was measuring his flour.

Brimhall got his tape measure. He went outside and measured the width of a footprint. He measured the length. When he came in, he said, "Know your enemy, Bear."

Still Bear didn't seem to hear. He was greasing his cake pans.

Brimhall went downstairs, came up with a shovel, and went outside again. An hour later he came back in. "I think we will catch him tonight," he said.

Bear paid no attention. He was frosting his cakes.

Chapter Three

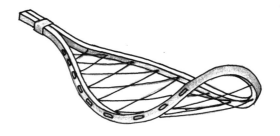

That night more snow fell. The cousins slept soundly in their warm beds. They didn't wake up until late the next morning.

Brimhall ran to the door. "Bear, there are fresh footprints! Brand new fresh footprints."

Brimhall followed them out the door. He came back in a few minutes.

"I didn't catch him," he said sadly. "I dug a huge hole and covered it with leaves, but he isn't there."

"Maybe he is a friendly animal, Brimhall," said Bear. "Maybe we don't have to catch him."

"Anything this large, Bear, is dangerous," said Brimhall. "Why, he is three times the size of you, and you are a large bear."

That evening Brimhall went to check his trap again. There was nothing in it. The next morning he looked, but all he saw was a deep, empty hole. There was nothing in the hole that afternoon either.

"Tonight I am going to sit up all night and wait," said Brimhall. "I won't miss this animal tonight, Bear."

Brimhall sat down and put his feet on the footstool. Soon he was asleep.

Bear put a pot of stew on the stove for dinner. Suddenly he heard a tap-tap-tap at the door.

Bear opened the door. "Why, Roger!" he said. "What are you doing out in this deep snow? How did you get here?"

"On my snowshoes, Bear. Look."

Bear looked down at Roger's feet. Then he looked at the large tracks the snowshoes had made in the snow.

"Why, Roger!" said Bear. "I believe *you* are Brimhall's monster! He has been trying to catch you, Roger. He thinks you are a giant animal."

"Me?" said Roger. "A monster?" The two friends began to laugh.

Just then Brimhall woke up. "Hello, Roger," he said. Then he noticed the snowshoes. "What's that on your feet?"

"Snowshoes," said Roger.

Brimhall looked at the snowshoes. Then he looked outside at the tracks. "Roger, have you been coming to our door wearing those snowshoes?"

"Yes," said Roger. "I've come several times, but no one answered. I think your doorbell must be broken."

"Well, feature that," said Brimhall, rubbing his chin. "So you are our monster. You certainly had us fooled."

Roger took off his snowshoes and set them next to the door.

Brimhall picked them up and looked at them.

"Do you mind if I try out your snowshoes, Roger?"

"Go ahead," said Roger.

Brimhall put on the snowshoes and walked down the road. "Look!" he called as he walked on top of a snow-drift. "I am the tallest bear in the forest!" he sang as he walked over the top of a fence. "Look at meeee!" he shouted as he fell—right into his own trap. "HELP!" he cried.

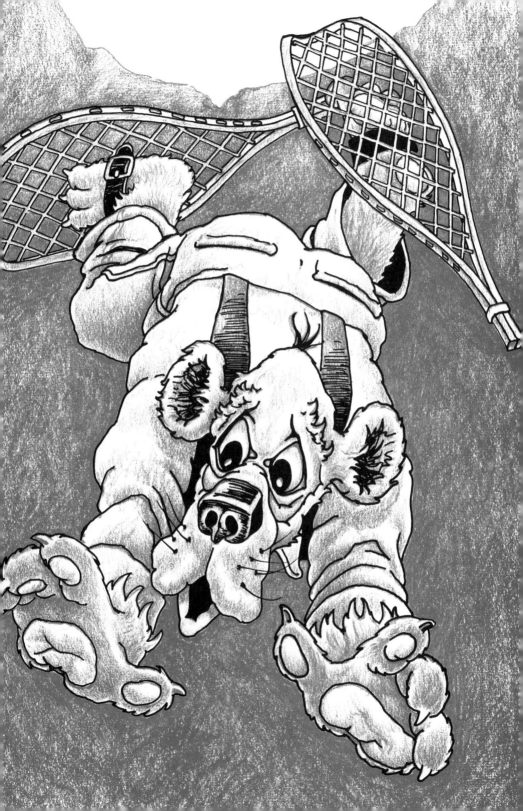

Roger and Bear rushed outside to
the large hole.

"Well, Brimhall," said Bear after he
and Roger had pulled Brimhall out,
"at last you caught something in your
trap."

Chapter Four

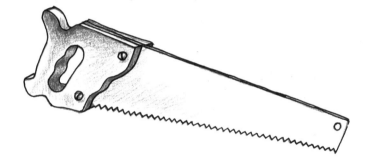

Bear and Roger laughed and laughed. But Brimhall was not laughing. He was blushing.

"This trap could have saved us, Bear," he said. "There *could* have been a dangerous monster, you know."

"You had better fill up the hole, Brimhall," said Bear, "before you trap anyone else in the woods."

But Brimhall seemed to have his mind on something else.

44

"Have you been to Raccoon's lately, Roger?" he asked. "Does he know about your snowshoes?"

"Why, no," said Roger.

"Hmmm," said Brimhall.

"Let's play a game of chess before dinner, Roger," invited Bear.

"Fine," said Roger.

The three friends went into the house, and Bear made a pot of tea. Then he and Roger sat down at the chessboard. The snow was falling gently in the woods. From downstairs in the basement came the sound of a saw cutting wood.

"Brimhall?" called Bear as he waited for Roger to make his move. "Brimhall, what are you doing down there?"

46

"Er . . . nothing, Bear," came the
answer. "Just . . . ah . . . working with
some pieces of wood."

48